This book belongs to

. . . .

I celebrated World Book Day 2016 with this
brilliant gift from my local Bookseller and
Penguin Random House UK Children's!

DAISY
and the TROUBLE with
JACK

Have you read these other troublesome tales all about me?

And look out for
the first ever
story all about me!

JACK BEECHWHISTLE:
ATTACK OF THE GIANT SLUGS

JACK

and the TROUBLE with

DAISY

by Kes Gray

Illustrated by Garry Parsons

RED FOX

RED FOX

UK | USA | Canada | Ireland | Australia
India | New Zealand | South Africa

Red Fox is part of the Penguin Random House group of companies
whose addresses can be found at global.penguinrandomhouse.com.

www.penguin.co.uk
www.puffin.co.uk
www.ladybird.co.uk

First published by Red Fox in 2016

001

Set in VAG Rounded Light 15/23pt
Printed in Great Britain by Clays Ltd, St Ives plc

A CIP catalogue record for this book is available from the British Library

ISBN: 978–1–782–95630–3

All correspondence to:
Red Fox
Penguin Random House Children's
80 Strand, London WC2R 0RL

Penguin Random House is committed to a sustainable future for our business, our readers
and our planet. This book is made from Forest Stewardship Council® certified paper.

To as many words as you can make out of

I LOVE WORLD BOOK DAY!

(Including K.G.

But not including INCLUDING.

Or

I.

Or

LOVE.

Or

WORLD.

Or

BOOK.

Or

DAY!)

The **trouble** **with** **Jack** **Beechwhistle** is he's a boy.

The **trouble with boys** is they are so immature, apart from

my friend Dylan. Dylan is a boy who lives in my street. He's not immature at all, because he's ten. Jack Beechwhistle isn't ten, he's about two. Well, he acts about two.

Do you know what Jack Beechwhistle keeps telling everyone at school? That he is a secret agent. How silly is that? I mean, if he's a secret agent, how come he can't keep it a secret?!

Jack says that the only reason we are safe is because of him, like he's some kind of world super children protector or something. If he's such a world super children protector and everything, how come I've seen his bottom?

I have seen his bottom, you know – cross my heart and hope to die. I saw it when I was fishing with my Uncle Clive. Jack was canoeing down the same river when he accidentally got some of my fishing maggots in his pants.

Jack says I fired maggots at him on purpose with a catapult, but that's not true. It wasn't a catapult, it was a magapult. Which is different. And anyway, he shouldn't have stuck his tongue out at me as he went past.

5

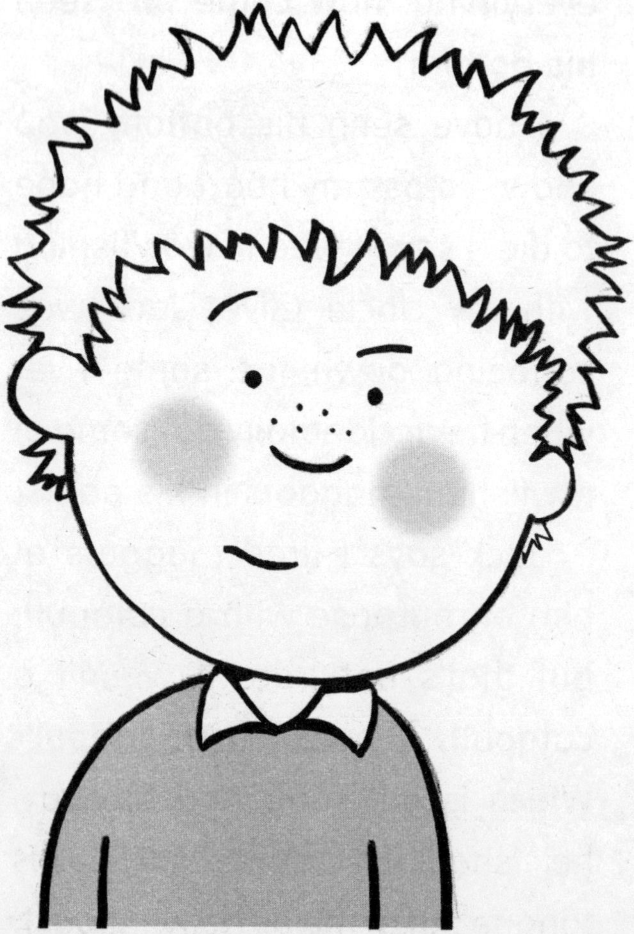

The **trouble with Daisy Butters** is she's a girl.

The trouble with girls is they are soft in the head. Apart from Violet in *The Incredibles*.

She's not soft in the head at all, because she's got super powers. If girls had super powers, they would be really cool. But they haven't. All they are is super soft.

Do you know what Daisy Butters keeps telling everyone at school? She keeps telling them that one day she is either going to be prime minister or an ice-cream man. Or BOTH! I mean, how daft is that? How can she be an ice-cream *man* if she's a girl, plus how can a prime minister go round the street selling ice creams?!

Daisy says it's a really good way of getting votes, especially if you give all the ice creams away. But I say, if you put a prime minister in an ice-cream van it will be a risk to national security. A sniper could take him out just like that, because he'll be standing by a wide open window when he gives out the lollies. Plus he won't have any bodyguards to save him, because six bodyguards and a prime minister won't fit into an ice-cream van. Especially if they need to do Ninja skills.

Jack Beechwhistle is the biggest fibber I know. In fact, he tells so many fibs I'm surprised his tongue hasn't fallen off.

Do you know what he told me and my best friend Gabby this morning? He told us that he had been brought up by wolves. WOLVES?! Monkeys, more like.

And he told us that his dad owns a tank.

The **trouble with fibs** is they can get other people in trouble.

Especially if you tell the person who's telling the fibs he's a fibber.

Gabby and me told Jack that if his dad has a tank, then he should prove it by bringing it into school. But Jack said it was only allowed to be used for military purposes.

The **trouble with military purposes** is you're not allowed to bring military anything into

school, a bit like chewing gum and coloured socks.

When we told Jack that we still didn't believe him about the tank, he said we should ask his best friends Harry and Colin because they would totally back him up.

Which wasn't a fib, because

they both did.

But then they said they were brought up by wolves too.

Which meant that now all three of them were fibbing.

The **trouble with three people fibbing** is it makes you really cross, especially when there are only two of you.

I said that if Jack, Harry and Colin were totally brought up by wolves, then they should prove it to me and Gabby by talking in "wolf" language.

The **trouble with talking in "wolf" language** is wolves don't talk. They only howl.

The **trouble with howls** is you're not allowed to bring those into school either.

But Jack suddenly did. Right in the middle of the classroom, just as Mrs Peters came in to take the morning register.

Mrs Peters is our teacher. Trouble is, she was brought up by T. Rexes.

Daisy Butters is the biggest telltale I know. In fact, she tells so many tales I'm surprised her tongue hasn't split.

Every time I do anything in class that is even the slightest bit fun, she tells Mrs Peters.

If I turn my pen into a peashooter and *blow* pieces of chewed-up paper at her, she *blabs*.

If I throw the tiniest piece of my rubber at her head, she *blabs*.

Even once when I put a really cute earwig in her school bag, she *blabbed*.

The **trouble with blabbing** is it can get other people into trouble.

Me, Colin and Harry would never blab on anyone. Apart from Daisy and Gabriella.

The **trouble with Daisy and Gabriella** is they think they're always right, even when they're wrong.

When me, Colin and Harry told them we were brought up by wolves, we didn't actually say "totally" brought up by wolves, we just said "brought up by wolves". Which doesn't necessarily mean all the time – it could just mean after school and at weekends. And not every weekend either; only the times when we go to the Dark Dark Wood.

The **trouble with the Dark Dark Wood** is it's a place that girls would never dare to go. Because not only are

there wild wild wolves there, there's a mad mad tramp living there too, deep deep deep in the heart of the forest.

A lot of people think that the mad mad tramp was brought up by wolves too. I'm still trying to find out if that is true. It's not going to be easy though. I'm going to have to use all of my tracking skills and everything.

The **trouble with tracking skills** is if you haven't got them, you will never *be able* to creep up on the mad mad tramp.

Even if you track him in the dark.

The mad mad tramp doesn't trust humans. His only friends are woodland animals. Me, Harry and Colin have tried to make contact loads of times because we want to learn his forest skills. So far I haven't managed to see even a glimpse of him.

I have *seen* a mad mad Mrs Peters, though.

As soon as Mrs Peters came into the classroom, she went loopy. She doesn't like people doing wolf howls in class. Especially werewolf howls.

If I had known Mrs Peters had come into the classroom I'd have stopped looking at Jack and everything. Trouble is, I had my back to her when she walked in.

The **trouble with having your back to a teacher** is they can't see what your lips are doing.

Honestly, the only thing my lips were doing was the tiniest bit of smiling. I wasn't doing any wolf noises at all. But Jack said I was!

Not only that, he said he was only doing wolf noises because I had asked him to!

When Mrs Peters asked Gabby if it was true, Gabby had to say that it was. Because it was.

That's the trouble with Gabby; she always tells the truth.

Unlike Jack Beechwhistle!

As soon as Mrs Peters folded her arms I knew she was going to tell us off, so I told her it was Jack who had been doing all the wolf noises. Just in case she thought me and Gabby had been doing it too.

I couldn't believe what Jack Beechwhistle told Mrs Peters next.

He said I'd asked him to do HIPPO noises too! Which is an absolute LIE!

I've never even talked to a hippopotamus, so how would I even know what kind of noises a hippopotamus makes?!

Mrs Peters wasn't even listening when I told her that Jack had said he was brought up by wolves. She said she didn't want to hear another word from either Jack or me for the rest of the day, apart from "Here, miss" when she took the register.

There were loads of words I wanted to say, and none of them were nice ones. Especially when Mrs Peters told Jack that he had to swap places with Gabby and sit in the actual chair next to mine.

AT MY ACTUAL DESK!

When I saw Mrs Peters come into the classroom I had to think really quickly, because I was halfway through a werewolf howl.

The trouble with werewolf howls is they are really loud, especially if you are giving it all you've got.

There was no point in pretending that I hadn't been doing the howling because Mrs Peters had seen me.

So I decided that if I was going to get told off, then Daisy Butters might as well get told off too.

Daisy had no idea that Mrs Peters was standing right behind her because she had her back to the classroom door.

So did Gabriella.

By the time Gabriella gave Daisy a nudge, it was too late. Because the whole class had gone quiet by then.

Even I had gone quiet, and I never go quiet in class usually. Quiet isn't really my thing. I mean, if you've got a voice and you are really good at doing animal impressions, especially wild animal impressions, then why not use it?

The trouble with quiet is it makes a teacher's voice sound even scarier.

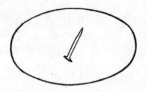

"What is the meaning of this?" Mrs Peters said. "Have I walked into a classroom this morning or have I walked into a zoo?"

"IT WAS HIM!" said Daisy, before Mrs Peters even had a chance to fold her arms.

"It wasn't me or Gabby doing the wolf noises. It was Jack!" she blabbed. "He says he's been brought up by wolves!"

As soon as I saw Daisy's finger
pointing at me, I knew exactly what I
needed to do.

So I pointed at her too.

"IT WASN'T ME, IT WAS DAISY!"
I said. "I was sitting really quietly at
my desk, minding my own business,
when Daisy came in and asked me if
I knew how to do wolf noises. AND
HIPPO NOISES!" I said.

You should have seen Daisy's face.
It was hilarious. I think her mouth
opened wider than a hippo's!

Mrs Peters didn't know who to
believe. Especially when Daisy folded
her arms and went all sulky.

She went even sulkier when I folded my arms and went all sulky back.

The trouble with three people folding their arms at the same time

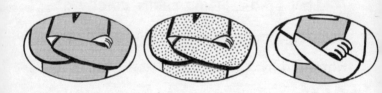

is it looks a bit silly, so Mrs Peters put her hands on her hips instead.

She said she didn't want to hear another sound from either of us for the rest of the day.

Which was a shame really, because I was going to tell her that Daisy had asked me to do kookaburra noises too. And hyena noises and the sound of a gorilla flushing a toilet in a jungle.

I wish I had now, because do you know what Mrs Peters said next?

It was the worst punishment you could give on Earth. Or Mars. Or any planet in the Solar System.

She said instead of going back to my desk, I had to swap places with Gabriella and sit next to DAISY!

There's only one thing worse than sitting next to a boy in class, and that's sitting next to a boy in class called Jack Beechwhistle.

When Mrs Peters told me I had to make room for the worst boy in the world I nearly threw my fluffy pencil case at the wall. There are only two chairs at my desk and the chair next to me is only meant for Gabby!

When Jack sat down next to me, he gave me one of his funny looks. So I gave him one of my funny looks back.

Then he gave me two funny looks, so I gave him about five.

Then Mrs Peters looked at us, so we had to stop.

Which meant I won.

There's only one thing worse than sitting next to a girl in class, and that's sitting next to a girl in class called Daisy Butters.

When Mrs Peters told me I had to swap places with Gabriella Summers, I nearly threw my chair through the classroom window. I'd rather sit in a puddle of rhino wee than on the same desk as Daisy Butters.

Mrs Peters said that if Daisy and I sat next to each other, it would be easier for her to keep an eye on the two of us. How rubbish is that? I mean, what is the point of a teacher having two eyes if she can't use them to look in two directions at once?

When I sat down next to Daisy, she gave me one of her looks, so I gave her one of my looks back. Then she gave me two of her looks, so I gave her three of my looks back. Then Mrs Peters looked at us, so we had to stop.

Which meant I'd won.

After Mrs Peters had called the register, she told me and Jack that the only noises we were allowed to make from now on were giraffe noises. Which sounded quite good fun at first. But then Mrs Peters told us that giraffes don't have voices. They can't make any noises at all. Apparently they can't even squeak.

I don't know why giraffes don't have voices. Maybe it's because they have spent too many millions of years showing off to all the other animals.

"Hey, lion, look up here! I'm

way, way taller than you!"

"Oi, alligator! Look up here! What's the weather like down there?"

"Hey, shortcake! Look up here! You should see the view from where I am. It's absolutely brilliant!"

"Hey, titch, look up here, I'm eating really high-up leaves and they're really juicy!! Don't you wish you could reach high-up leaves just like me?"

After about a trillion years I reckon the giraffes ran out of animals to tell how tall they were, so their voices ran out too. A bit like getting a sore throat for ever.

If I was a giraffe and I got a sore throat for ever, I'd go to a really high-up sweet shop and ask for some long-lasting cough sweets.

I wonder if giraffes make a noise when they are sucking?

I'm not sure what flavour cough sweet I'd choose because 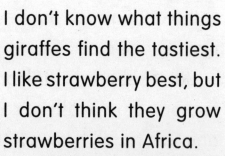 I don't know what things giraffes find the tastiest. I like strawberry best, but I don't think they grow strawberries in Africa.

I guess leaf flavour would be best for a

giraffe, or maybe banana flavour, because bananas are so long.

Whatever flavour I chose, there is one person I definitely wouldn't

share any of my cough sweets with, though – or any of my normal sweets.

Jack Beechwhistle!

I don't know why giraffes don't have voices; I need to look it up on the internet. It's probably because their necks are too stretched.

If I was a full-time giraffe and I couldn't speak, I'd get one of those computerized voices that Sir Stephen Hawking has got. They are totally cool, because they make you sound like a robot.

If you were a giraffe and you sounded like a robot, you would totally rule the jungle. If you could get the tufty bits on your head adapted to fire laser beams, you could probably take over the world.

I know exactly who I would fire my laser beams at if I was a robot giraffe. The same person I ping my rubber bands at. Daisy Butters.

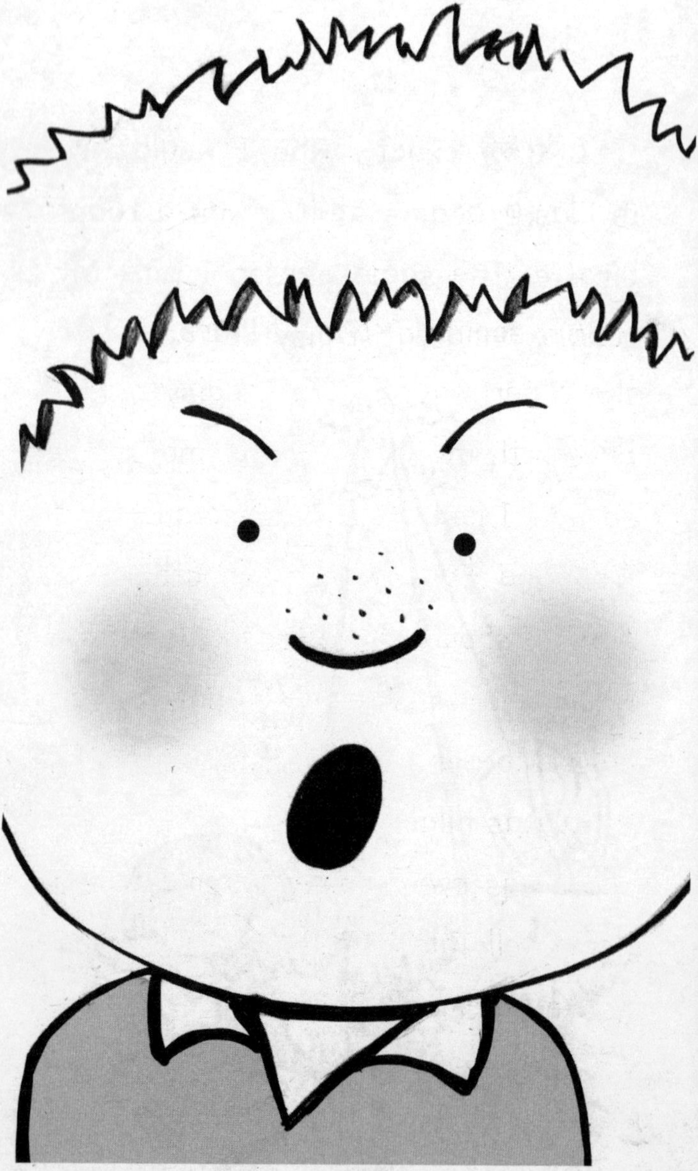

Anyhow, just *because* giraffes can't speak, it doesn't mean they can't move their lips!

As soon as Mrs Peters looked the other way, I called Daisy a Poo Face with my lips. I didn't make any sounds, I just stared at her and went 'Poo' and 'Face' with my mouth.

You should have seen her face when she worked out what I was saying to her.

It was hilarious!

It was even funnier when I called her a Tell Tale.

And a Sneak Chops.

And a Baboon Features!

I absolutely couldn't believe my eyes when Jack Beechwhistle started talking to me in giraffe language. I knew it was giraffe language because he was moving his lips on purpose but he wasn't making any sounds.

The **trouble with someone talking giraffe language at you** is all you can do is watch their lips and try and work out what they are saying.

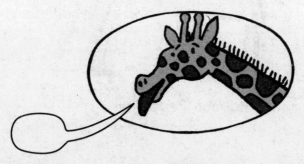

It made me so cross!

First he called me a Poo Face.

Then he called me a Towel Flau.

Then he called me a Snail Drops.

And then I think he called me a Boo Boo Face Mask!

All when Mrs Peters wasn't looking!

The trouble with Mrs Peters not looking is when I called Jack

a 'Bogey Bum Bot' in revenge, she WAS looking.

Because she looked round at just the wrong time. Which meant she saw my lips moving up and down in Jack's direction instead of Jack's lips moving up and down in my direction. Which was so unfair, because Jack was the one who did the giraffe language first.

Except now Jack Beechwhistle wasn't even looking at me at all! Now he was looking at his French book!

He is such a sneak!

One of the first skills you learn as a junior world defence agent is to never get caught.

When Mrs Peters saw Daisy calling me a Pooey Bum Pot I did what all junior world defence agents are trained to do: I started writing in my French book straight away.

Daisy was furious, but she couldn't do anything about it. She couldn't even move her lips at me! Because Mrs Peters was still watching. All she could do was fold her arms.

As soon as Mrs Peters looked away again, I gave Daisy another of my looks. Only now she'd stolen MY idea of pretending to be interested in a French book as well!

The **trouble with French books** is they are full of words that don't make sense.

So I knew it wouldn't be long before Daisy looked at me again.

Except she didn't. She just kept staring at her French book. And staring and staring and staring!!!

Even when I gave her a jog with my elbow, she kept staring at her French book.

Even when I gave her a nudge with my knee, she kept ignoring me.

The **trouble with someone totally ignoring me** is it makes me totally determined to make them stop.

So I thought of a sound that a giraffe really *could* make!

When Jack did a trump in class it was so loud I nearly fell off my chair! It sounded like he had a trombone under the desk!

The **trouble with trombones** is you aren't allowed to bring them into school either. Even for

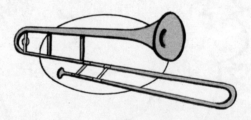

music lessons we're only allowed to bring recorders or violins, so there was no way Mrs Peters wasn't going to notice a noise like that.

As soon as she heard Jack's trump, she looked straight at my desk to see who was to blame.

Trouble is, Jack was looking at his French book again! And now he was pretending to do writing! Which meant that I was the only one out of the two of us who was laughing! (Not including the rest of the class, but Mrs Peters wasn't looking at them.)

The **trouble with laughing** is you're not allowed to do it during lessons.

Or before lessons. Or after lessons. Especially in Mrs Peters' classroom. You're only allowed to do laughing in the playground. (Except on the quiet bench.)

As soon as Mrs Peters saw me laughing in class, she went really frowny. Luckily, when she saw Jack reading his French book and doing writing, she got really suspicious. I'm not sure she'd ever seen him do either of those things before. Not at the same time, anyway.

I'm sure Jack thought he wasn't going to get caught, but

he did! Because teachers know absolutely everything about boys like Jack Beechwhistle.

So he got told to go and stand beside Mrs Peters' desk and face the class!

It was so funny!

Until I got told to go and stand at the front of the class too.

Standing up in front of the class doesn't really bother me – I've done it so many times before.

être   avoir

suis   ai
es
est
    av_ _ _ _
_ _ _ mes

If you ask me, having to stand beside Mrs Peters' desk is a hundred times better than having to sit down and do reading and writing.

The best thing about it is, it gives me secret thinking time to plan the next training mission I'm going to do with Colin and Harry. Me, Colin and Harry go on training missions after school all the time, and at weekends. I'm teaching them to be world defence agents like me.

To be a junior world defence agent you need to learn loads of skills - not just survival skills but combat skills too. I've already shown them how to cook bacon. And whittle sticks. I'm teaching them how to do double headlocks too.

I had a really good view of Harry and Colin from the front of the class. Poor old Harry had Gabriella Summers sitting next to him instead of me. Thanks to Daisy.

The **trouble with sitting next to Gabriella Summers** is you have to be really careful what you say, because

she's a blabber too. Give away any secrets to Gabriella, and you can bet your life she will tell them straight to Daisy.

Tell secrets to Daisy and she will tell them to the whole wide world.

Well, she would do if she wasn't standing at the front of the class going red!

Standing up at the front of the class is sooooo embarrassing. Especially when you haven't done anything wrong. This morning was the first time it has ever

happened to me in my entire life – apart from the other times it happened to me, which weren't my fault either.

The trouble with standing up at the front of the class is it makes your cheeks go really hot.

Because while you are facing the class you can see everyone looking straight at you. And laughing in secret at you. And giggling in secret at you.

Except for Gabby. Gabby would never do anything in secret at me, because we're best friends forever. And anyway, she had nothing to laugh or giggle about because she had Harry Bayliss sitting next to her. Thanks to Jack.

The **trouble with people laughing and giggling in secret at you** is it makes you want to go to the loo.

Well, it made me want to go to the loo. Really really badly.

The **trouble with wanting to go to the loo really really badly** is it's really really difficult to ask if you're not allowed to speak.

In fact, it's absolutely impossible. All you can do is hold up your hand and wait for Mrs Peters to notice you.

The trouble with holding up your hand and waiting for Mrs Peters to notice you is it makes it look like you know the answer to a question.

Which was really unlucky, because I was so busy concentrating on crossing my legs, I had no idea that a question had even been asked!

When Mrs Peters said, "Yes, Daisy, the answer is . . ." I went even hotter. Because not only didn't I know what the answer was, I didn't know what the question was either. Because I hadn't been listening. I was too busy being cross with Jack Beechwhistle.

I would never have put my hand up if I'd realized Mrs Peters had asked a question. I would have kept my hand down. Especially if it was a French question. But it was too late.

When Mrs Peters said,

"Permission to speak," I went even hotter still, because all I could think of to say was: "Please can I go to the toilet?"

When I said, "Please can I go to the toilet?" everyone in the class burst out laughing. Not because I wanted to go to the toilet but because apparently Mrs Peters' question had been, "What does 'Quelle heure est-il?' mean in English?"

Apparently it means "What is the time?" but I didn't know that because I've only learned up to "un, deux, trois", plus I'm not French, double plus the only French I'm good at is French skipping.

Mrs Peters wasn't impressed.

Watching Daisy Butters make a fool of herself in front of the whole class was hilarious! She didn't know the answer to Mrs Peters' question *because* she hadn't been listening! From the look on her face she didn't even know what the question was! Trouble was, neither did I *because* I hadn't been listening either. I had been planning a zombie assault mission in my head.

Zombie assault missions take a lot more thinking about than you would think. Especially when school keeps getting in the way.

During my secret thinking time I had decided that me, Colin and Harry were going to play zombie basketball at the weekend.

Basically, to play zombie basketball you have to run at a zombie, pull his head off and dunk it through a basketball hoop.

If you slam dunk the *basketball*, then the zombie is slam dead! If you miss the hoop, the zombie head grows into two more zombies! And the zombie wars grow! Colin has a *basketball* net on the back wall of his house, so I knew exactly where we could play. The only thing I still needed to work out was where to get some more balls from.

When everyone in the class suddenly started laughing at Daisy, I actually had no idea why they were laughing. So I decided that the best thing to do was pretend I did and just laugh along with them.

Trouble is, I think I must have laughed too loud, because instead of Mrs Peters frowning at Daisy, she started frowning at me. Not only that, she folded her arms again and gave me permission to speak too.

The **trouble with being given permission to speak too** is you totally have to say something, even if you don't know the answer either.

Or the question.

So I asked if I could go to the loo as well.

Mrs Peters wasn't too pleased.

Neither was Daisy.

When Jack Beechwhistle asked Mrs Peters if he could go to the loo too, I was so cross I wanted to stamp my foot! There was absolutely no way that Jack Beechwhistle really really wanted to go to the loo.

Or even really wanted to go to the loo.

Or even wanted to go to the loo.

He was only saying it to get out of answering the French question.

I wasn't. I was saying it because I really needed to go!

The **trouble with stamping your foot when you want to go to the loo** is it could actually make you go to the loo, right in front of the class.

Especially if you're desperate.

So I didn't, because I didn't want to wet myself.

Instead I gave Jack Beechwhistle the worst look I could absolutely turn my face into. Even if Mrs Peters was looking.

I didn't really want to go to the loo.
It was the only thing I could think of
to say.

Daisy did, though. She wanted to
go to the loo so bad, she had crossed
her legs twice!!

When she made a really stupid
face at me, right in front of Mrs
Peters, I crossed my legs on purpose
back at her, just to make her want to
go to the loo even more!

Trouble is, instead of letting Daisy
and me go to the loo, Mrs Peters
made us go to different corners of
the room and face the wall instead.

Until morning break!

When Mrs Peters made me and Jack go and face different corners of the classroom, I nearly fainted, I was so desperate to go to the

loo. But when I got there and got my legs crossed again, I was actually quite pleased. Because at least I didn't have to look at Jack Beechwhistle any more.

I'd much rather look at a wall than at Jack Beechwhistle.

By the time the bell went for morning break, I had my legs crossed, my arms crossed, my eyes crossed; I even had my ears crossed.

How I didn't do a puddle on the classroom floor I have no idea.

Jack Beechwhistle is sooooo infuriating!

Facing walls doesn't bother me in the slightest. All it does is give me more thinking time to plan other training missions with Colin and Harry.

Me, Colin and Harry go on training missions all the time. Mostly on our bikes.

If we didn't have to go to school, Harry and Colin would *be* fully trained world defence agents by now, *because* I'd have more time to teach them my skills.

I wouldn't *be* able to teach anything to anybody if I was sat next to Daisy Butters.

She is *so* annoying!

It was at least five minutes before me and Gabby got into the playground.

That's **the trouble with going to the loo at break time** – the queues.

Especially the queues for the girls' loos.

As soon as we got to the drinking fountain, we spotted Jack Beechwhistle. He was over by the climbing frames with Colin and Harry.

"There they are," I said, giving Gabby a nudge. "Don't look at them – pretend we haven't seen them."

"Let's go and sit on the quiet bench," whispered Gabby. "It's a totally Jack-free zone."

Gabby was right: if Jack

Beechwhistle sat on a quiet bench, he'd probably drop down dead, because "quiet" is something he doesn't know how to do. Unless Mrs Peters makes him.

Barry Morely does, though.

Barry Morely is the quietest and cleverest boy in our class; he's probably the cleverest person in our whole school. He never gets into trouble, he never gets questions wrong; in fact, he is so clever he writes with a fountain pen.

Fountain pens aren't like normal pens. They have really posh nibs that do inkier writing, plus they come with special plastic tubes full of blue ink.

You have to be an actual genius to use an actual fountain pen.

The **trouble with Barry Morely** is he always sits on the quiet bench, mostly on his own.

Which means that if you sit on the quiet bench too, you really have to talk to him. Otherwise you're not being friendly and kind.

He's actually really nice when you get to know him, unless he's telling you "interesting facts".

The **trouble with interesting facts** is sometimes they make me and Gabby yawn.

Because sometimes interesting facts can actually be quite boring.

This morning was totally different, though! This morning Barry Morely told me and Gabby a fact that was so interesting and so unusual and so GIRAFFEY, it gave me the most GENIUS idea!

Not only that; it was a genius idea that would help me put Jack Beechwhistle totally in his place!

As soon as the *bell* went for morning break, I called an emergency meeting with Colin and Harry. Well, as soon as Mrs Peters let me and Daisy out of our corners, I called an emergency meeting with Colin and Harry.

First I wanted to tell them about zombie basketball. Second I wanted to tell them not to be friends with Daisy and Gabriella. Even if they tried to be friends with us.

Harry said he didn't have any basketballs at home, but he could bring a football to use as a zombie's head. Colin said if we fought zombie children too, we could use tennis balls as heads as well. Then we decided to add a zombie weasel because I remembered I had a golf ball in my bedroom drawer.

It was at least five minutes before Daisy and Gabriella came out into the playground, which was handy actually, because zombie basketball is a far more exciting thing to talk about than two annoying girls.

"Here they come," I said as they

walked past the drinking fountain. "Don't look at them, though. Pretend we haven't seen them."

Daisy had her legs uncrossed so she must have been to the loo.

Gabriella's legs had been uncrossed all morning, so I couldn't tell if she'd been as well.

As soon as they looked in our direction, we looked away. There was no way we were going to talk to them, even if they came right over to where we were standing.

Which they didn't.

They went over to the quiet bench to talk to Barry Morely instead.

The **trouble with watching** Gabriella **Summers and Daisy Butters talking to Barry Morely** is it makes you want to know what they are saying.

Barry Morely is really smart; in fact, he is so smart I was thinking of asking him if he wanted to train to be a junior world defence agent too. Super intelligence is a really good skill to have if you want to be a world defence agent. Trouble is, I don't think he'd be any good at survival or combat.

Plus there's only enough room for three agents in our secret den.

The more me, Harry and Colin watched Barry Morely talking to Daisy and Gabriella, the more suspicious we got.

If I'd brought in some of my world defence bugging devices, I could have rigged up the bench and listened to every word they were saying. But all my secret microphones were at home.

When Barry reached into his school bag and gave Daisy something, I got even more suspicious.

When Daisy went back to class before the school bell had actually rung, I totally knew that she was up to something.

I needed to talk to Barry.

The trouble with quiet benches is they are benches where you have to be quiet.

Which is why I've been banned from them since Year Two.

Normally I wouldn't go anywhere near a quiet bench, but if Daisy was up to something, then I needed to know what it was. So I risked it.

I think Barry was really surprised when I sat down next to him. I don't think he'd spoken to two people in one break before.

He's actually really nice when you get to know him. Plus he's full of really interesting facts. Including facts about GIRAFFES!

When he told me his most amazing fact about giraffes, it didn't just amaze me, it gave me a really brilliant idea. Not just that; it was an idea that would help me put Daisy Butters totally in her place!

DID YOU KNOW THAT GIRAFFES HAVE BLUE TONGUES? I didn't – Barry Morely told me! At first I thought he was joking, but Barry Morely doesn't do jokes. So it must be true.

Maybe it's all the blue cough sweets they've been sucking.

As soon as I found out that giraffes have blue tongues, I knew exactly how to get my own back on Jack Beechwhistle.

Even better still, he wouldn't be expecting it one bit!

I had called Jack a Bogey Bum

Bot in giraffe language, now I was going to poke my tongue out at him in giraffe too!

All I needed to do was persuade Barry Morely to help.

The trouble with poking your tongue out in giraffe is you need to make your tongue blue.

Not your lips, though, or it won't be a surprise.

Luckily Barry Morely said he'd swap one of his ink cartridges for my strawberry gel pen, so suddenly I had all the blue ink that I needed!

As soon as I got the ink from Barry I raced back to class with Gabby. At first we weren't sure how to get the ink out, but once we pricked the end of the tube with a compass it was really easy!

I stuck my tongue out; Gabby did the colouring. The taste was disgusting and I think I might have nearly poisoned myself but it was totally worth it.

All I had to do now was wait for Jack Beechwhistle!

DID YOU KNOW THAT GIRAFFES HAVE BLUE TONGUES? I didn't – Barry Morely told me, so it's definitely true.

My guess was giraffes have blue tongues because they live at high altitude. Things get really blue at high altitude. Because it's so cold.

But Barry said it was a different reason altogether. Apparently giraffe tongues are blue because it stops them getting sunburnt! How cool is that!

And that wasn't all that Barry knew about giraffes either!

Did you know a giraffe's tongue is the length of about one and a half rulers?

Did you know that no two giraffes have the same pattern on them?

Did you know that a giraffe's feet are the size of a dinner plate?

And did you know that giraffes give birth standing up? Which means their babies fall two metres to the ground when they are born!!!!!

I didn't know that either! But I do now, thanks to Barry Morely. Honestly, I'd learned more in five minutes with Barry Morely than I had in a whole term with Mrs Peters.

There aren't many people who can teach me things because I know so much already. Especially about the important things in life, like building dens, and damming streams, and climbing trees.

I bet Mrs Peters has never climbed a tree. I bet she's never even climbed a bush. I bet she couldn't even climb a blade of grass. Not without a stepladder anyway.

If you ask me, teachers shouldn't be allowed to be teachers unless they've done an assault course first. And wrestled a bear.

If he could learn to wrestle bears I reckon Barry Morely would make a brilliant teacher one day. He could even become prime minister, probably, he's so full of interesting facts.

Trouble is, when I got back to class I wasn't sitting next to Barry. I was sitting next to Daisy.

The **trouble with me and Jack** is we're too different.

I'm well behaved, he's not.

I listen in class, he doesn't.

I don't fall off my chair, he does.

I would never ping something at someone, he would.

In fact, we couldn't be more different!

The **trouble with me and Daisy** is we're too different.

She's a *blabber*, I'm not.

She would never wrestle a bear, I would.

She could never save the school from an alien attack, I could.

She likes *fluffy* pencil cases, I don't.

In fact, we couldn't *be* more different!

Trouble is, when I poked my new blue giraffe tongue out at Jack (BECAUSE HE TOTALLY DESERVED IT), Mrs Peters treated us both the same:

Trouble is, when I poked my new blue giraffe tongue out at Daisy (BECAUSE SHE TOTALLY DESERVED IT), Mrs Peters treated us both the same:

"The headmaster will see you now."

Which was so annoying! I couldn't believe a boy could have the same idea as me!

"The headmaster will see you now."

Which was so annoying! I couldn't believe a girl could have the same idea as me!

There was no way I was saying sorry to Jack.

There was no way I was saying sorry to Daisy.

'The headmaster will see you now.'

We did feel sorry for Barry Morely, though.

Daisy and Jack's Trouble Index

WORLD BOOK DAY *fest*

WORLD
**BOOK
DAY**
2 MARCH 2016

 Want to **READ** more?

 VISIT

YOUR LOCAL BOOKSHOP

- Get some great recommendations for what to read next
- Meet your favourite authors & illustrators at brilliant events
- Discover books you never even knew existed!

 FIND YOUR LOCAL BOOKSHOP www.booksellers.org.uk/bookshopsearch

 JOIN

YOUR LOCAL LIBRARY

You can browse and borrow from a HUGE selection of books and get recommendations of what to read next from expert librarians—all for **FREE**! You can also discover libraries' wonderful children's and family reading activities.

 FIND YOUR LOCAL LIBRARY www.findalibrary.co.uk

GET ONLINE

VISIT **WORLDBOOKDAY.COM** TO DISCOVER A WHOLE NEW WORLD OF BOOKS!

- Downloads and activities for top books and authors
- Cool games, trailers and videos
- Author events in your area
- News, competitions and new books—all in a FREE monthly email

AND MORE!